Untitled Finnish Comedy Project

Joni Järvi-Laturi

Kustantaja: BoD, Books on Demand, Helsinki, Suomi.
Valmistaja: BoD, Books on Demand, Norderstedt, Saksa.
ISBN: 978-952-80-4819-0

Part 2

PART 1

The Facebook Couple

As the interviewer interviews, pictures of the couple's Facebook posts and pictures are seen on the screen. The pictures are so sugary that it is annoying.

INTERVIEWER
Hello and welcome to our show. With me is now a man who is a famous actor, a 70-year old legend whose wife is twenty years younger than him. Please welcome Adam Lime. Hello Adam.

ADAM
Hello, Steven.

INTERVIEWER
You and your wife have been called the masters of Facebook. You are very popular at Facebook. Why is this?

ADAM
I think it is because we share our stories and get people excited about ourselves.

INTERVIEWER
What is your message concerning Facebook?

ADAM
It is this: Why don't people love each other more? Me and my wife love each other and post about our happiness and love so that other human beings can enjoy them. I don't see anything bad about sharing our happiness to everyone.

INTERVIEWER
So you think yourselves as modern-day preachers of love?

ADAM
Yes, something like that.

INTERVIEWER
You and your wife both send approximately ten posts a day to Facebook. What are the contents of you and your wife's Facebook posts?

ADAM
Well we send our old pictures when we met and our honeymoon pictures in foreign countries and we treat Facebook as a diary so we tend to send everything about our

lives there. Every achievement and every dream and every thought. We also send pictures of our sons and daughters so everyone can see them.

INTERVIEWER
I see.

ADAM
We also send our cooking receipts and our history, when we were children or younger. There is no need to hide all this for privacy.

INTERVIEWER
Do you do this for charity or for inspiring people?

ADAM
No, we just want to get attention and glow in our pride every second of the day.

INTERVIEWER
I see...thank you for telling your real motive. God's thumb will like you...Now

The End.

No Woman Is a Comic Genius

Hey

What?

I am afraid.

Of what?

I am afraid there is a comic genius in my front yard.

Ok, let's check it out.

Oh, wait, it's a woman. False alarm.

Mr. Big Man

A bass riff plays at the back.

Mr. Big Man has a beard and he perpetually looks pissed off at something. He looks stern and serious.

NARRATOR
This is Mr. Big Man. He is a man's man, a macho man. A manly man who has all the male hobbies and interests. He is part of every male subculture.

Mr. Big Man is at a local store choosing food items to purchase.

NARRATOR
He hunts and eats all the animals there are. He once ate the eyeballs and testicles of a moose. He also collects cars and repairs them. He served in the military as a captain. He knows all the war strategies. He loves heavy metal music. He plays the guitar and bass. He frequently tattoos himself if he loses a bet. He also loves sports. He plays hockey and football, as well as baseball. He also wrestles and does karate. He is a man's man. He goes to the gym three times a week. He has over 2000 trustworthy friends and acquaintances. He also has eleven children and has been married to three women.

Mr. Big Man leaves the store.

NARRATOR
But he also has a secret hobby. A feminine side, if you will. Some days he collects flowers and dresses up as a woman. He calls himself Diana, after the princess. He sometimes dreams of men degrading him and him objecting to them. He does gay porn.

Mr. Big Man is shown frolicking and jumping like a girl in his living-room dressed up as a woman.

NARRATOR
But don't tell anyone about this. Mr. Big Man would kick your ass for it.

The bass riff plays at the back, Mr. Big Man stares at the camera confidently nodding.

The Painting Gorilla

In an interview, a woman talks about equality with a gorilla by her side. The gorilla stays silent. The interviewer is a female.

INTEVIEWER
Here with me is a woman, who has been called a hypocrite by the right. Please welcome Anna Linden.

WOMAN
Thank you, Lisa.

INTERVIEWER
You have been called a hypocrite because you don't recognize the crimes of immigrants. What is your take on this?

WOMAN
The right-wing in Europe is just a bunch of racist, lonely and bitter men that go too far in their rhetoric. I think it is a form of toxic masculinity. Hate speech is also real.

INTERVIEWER
I see. You have been a called a hypocrite also, because you write letters to prisoners. Many men have found this hypocritical and they say that you are coddling psychopaths. What is your answer to this?

WOMAN
Well, I think some people think that I am immoral but I am really just a woman who wants to heal men, all kinds of men.

INTERVIEWER
I see…

WOMAN
We need massive re-evaluation of our standards and values. We in the West are so backward. We need love. The equal treatment of people concerns us all.

INTERVIEWER
Why do you believe in equality? What is the greatest thing of it?

WOMAN
I think it is the protection of all people. Take political correctness, for example. I have been called a softener of language. They say that I don't like freedom of speech.

Well, I don't like political incorrectness and racism. I think the generalizations concerning gender are insulting and a form of toxic masculinity.

INTERVIEWER
Well, you have talked about equality for a while. By your side there is a gorilla. You have married this gorilla who paints. He is a painting gorilla.

WOMAN
Yes, he is. I love him very much. He is big and aggressive. So he protects me from the bad world.

INTERVIEWER
Have you considered what the gorilla thinks about these things?

WOMAN
I have tried to communicate with him. But he only throws things to the wall and breaks things. I must cure him for that.

INTERVIEWER
He is a rough gorilla. An aggressive gorilla. He looks very big.

WOMAN
He is very big.

INTERVIEWER
Might I touch him. He seems interesting.

WOMAN
Yes you can.

The interviewer touches the gorilla. The gorilla then tears her arm angrily.

INTERVIEWER
He is an angry gorilla.

WOMAN
Yes he is.

INTERVIEWER
Well, that is the end of this interview, I'm afraid. Thank you for watching our broadcast. In the next episode I will be interviewing a conservative man who is gay and atheist.

The Sitter

A young man sits on a chair with his arms entwined tight around his stomach. The camera stares at him from different angles. While the narrator talks, the young man is viewed from different kinds of chairs.

NARRATOR
He was there. He saw everything. He saw generations of men and women. He saw everyone, around him, growing and becoming who they were. He saw life, from different perspectives, he heard all kinds of conversations during those years.

He was there. He saw everything.

And he never did anything. He just sat there, for four decades. No one knows why he did this. But he did.

The End.

Mental Health League

NARRATOR
This is a football team. Consisting of people who have mental illness. But in this tournament it doesn't matter. Everyone is a winner. There are only four teams and three matches. The winner wins a trophy. Everyone gets an honorary diploma for existing, being there. Even though only one group can win.

NARRATOR
Let's look at the game.

NARRATOR
Teams are getting ready to play. The two teams consist of twenty players but five of them are only at the field at a time.

Ugly, drooling players play football against each other. They all howl like retards.

NARRATOR
The women who tend them in their communities are chanting and wishing their team will win. They support the players by shouting to each player what a great player he or she is. For just participating in the game.

The women chant.

NARRATOR
They receive a big reward for just existing.

One player scores. The women start celebrating among others.

THE WOMEN
We won! We won!

NARRATOR
There we have it. An achievement of no importance. An achievement which no one will remember ever. Ever. Ever.

A captain of the team stares at the camera with a trophy in his hand and howls like a retard.

Women Testing Men

INTERVIEWER
We are now in a custom house. This is a new groundbreaking institution which offers
women tests on who to select as their boyfriend and eventually their husband.

WOMAN
We are here in the custom house. We are very serious women.

WOMAN
Customs. Customs. Scary word isn't it?

The interviewer says nothing

INTERVIEWER
The woman is the leader of the institution and her mission is to test men. As many as
a hundred men go to this place. The custom house.

The woman shows the house to the interviewer.

WOMAN
Here we have a man who is insomniac. The reason is us, we prohibited him from
falling asleep.

WOMAN
We also test men for how unemotional they can be. We don't want soft, sensitive
men. A woman who knows her worth always chooses the strong man. Always. A
man should have a car and should not visit his mother quite often.

INTERVIEWER
I see. Do you test men in other ways as well?

WOMAN
Yeah, we have a shooting test, fitness test, muscle test, sense of humour test and a
test where I stare deep in the eyes of the man for about an hour. We also have a test
where I shoot the man either in the thigh or the knee and I study on how he reacts to
it – in a mannish way or in a girly way. We also have a traditional duty test which we
use to frighten the men by telling them how we are going to put objects to their rear
ends.

INTERVIEW
And how do we men get to test you women?

The room is full of women who say nothing.

WOMAN
Go away.

Des'ree

A seven year old girl Des'ree walks to the supermarket without her parents knowing.

The parents yell out her name: "Des'ree, Des'ree!"

The parents ask: "Where the fuck is she?"

The next day two men sing a song together to their new band.

Des'ree asks: "What? What do you sing? Please let me hear!"

The men walk quietly to the elevator. Des'ree is in front of them.

Des'ree asks: "Sing the song for me."

The men say nothing.

Des'ree gives the middle finger to them.

The next day one of the men is in the elevator again. The door is about to close until Des'ree presses the button again and again so the elevator door keeps opening. She lets go and the man gets to go to the top floor.

The next day the same man goes with the elevator to the front yard of the building.

Outside the building his leg gets trapped in a foothold trap and he yells of horror as the trap raises his leg and his leg is up in the air in the trap and his head is staring at the front yard.

Des'ree sees this from her family's apartment window and smiles wickedly.

A Cooking Show Which Doesn't Affect At All to the Amount of Hungry, Poor
People in the Developing World

HOST
Welcome! To a A Cooking Show Which Doesn't Affect At All to the Amount of
Hungry, Poor People in the Developing World. I'm your host, Steven Watkins.
Tonight we have a battle between North English dish and South English dish.

The contestants fry different kinds of meat on top of their distinctive tables.

HOST
Now we are in a hurry. The team 2 is almost ready to share us their cuisine. So here
in this non-political cooking show which doesn't affect at all to the amount of
hungry, poor people in the developing world we are all ready to take a look at the
cuisine.

WOMAN
This is shrimp with mustard and yolk. It also has a bit of lime and lemon juice.

The woman eats the shrimp with the sauce dropping from her mouth and says:
"Delicious!"

MAN
We have cooked our opposing food. It is cannelloni with rosemary and mozzarella
and feta cheese. This very unimportant, materialistic and ethnocentrical meal, a
globally and historically self-centered and uttely pointless dish is now soon to be
uselessly eaten by our too well-fed and too fat man – Ernie.

Ernie enters the room.

Ernie eats the cannelloni. He gives a thumbs up as a sign of a good meal.

Again, the woman eats the shrimp with the sauce dropping from her mouth and says:
"Delicious!"

Western Pain

A Super-intelligent Chinese villain has a British agent Mr. Harris in his torture
chamber.

CHINESE VILLAIN
I have created a new serum which makes everyone live eternally. An eternal life. I
have already used this serum on these four Chinese women. They never get old. They
have an eternal life.

The four Chinese women sit on chairs smiling to the British agent.

CHINESE VILLAIN
Now it is your day to die, Mr. Harris. Before that let me tell you my Asian invention.
Since I loathe and detest the world, we as in Chinese people will put the Western into
space and give them the serum for eternal life. Then we will torture them for
centuries. An eternal Western pain. The torture will never stop.

CHINESE VILLAIN
Do you have anything to say, Mr. Harris?

MR. HARRIS
Aah, do you like The Beatles?

CHINESE VILLAIN
Well, yes, as a matter of fact I like their earlier work sometimes better, but sometimes
the creative and the more profound later work is better. I mean, Lennon wrote so
many good tunes and I think his effort in the band was greatly missed. And I love the
drumming of Ringo Starr.

MR. HARRIS
Yes, he was underrated.

CHINESE VILLAIN
Yeah. I just don't like the way they manipulated him in some instances.

MR. HARRIS
Yeah, me too. But what about beer and food?

CHINESE VILLAIN
Yeah, Heineken is very good. Also Carlsberg and Guinness.

MR. HARRIS
Oh, I agree, they're delicious brands.

CHINESE VILLAIN
Yeah, man.

Individualistic Facebook Post with Independent Thoughts That No One in the Group Likes

HOST
Welcome to Individualistic Facebook post with independent thoughts that no one in the group likes.

OFF-SCREEN MEN
Individualistic Facebook post with independent thoughts that no one in the group likes.

OFF-SCREEN MEN
Individualistic Facebook post with independent thoughts that no one in the group likes.

HOST
This Facebook post was posted live last Wednesday in a group of musicians. Let us see how the group handled with it. The post was written by a struggling musician who searched for the right person to compose songs with him. The group doesn't like clear visions for music. The group also hates individuality and independent thoughts. They want music to be fun and without clear goals for anything. Here are the group's reactions on live Facebook.

A group of hundred people stand in front of the struggling musician's house and yell out mean comments to him while he is watching the group from the window of his balcony.

MAN IN THE CROWD
You should re-think your priorities, man. That post was too long and had too many selfish points. You seem like a self-centered, snobbish dork with so many demands for your composer.

The musician opens the front door.

The crowd laughs and point fingers to the musician. Then one of the crowd members puts a laughing emoji to the musician's head.

WOMAN IN THE CROWD
I really don't like what you said. You are self-centered. It is like you search for some kind of a perfect composer. I have been in the music business for a long time and I really don't see a good future before you.

THE MUSICIAN
Ok, sorry. I didn't know that having my own thoughts and my own visions was so offensive to your Facebook group. But might we please try to understand each others more and try to listen to one another a bit more without all the judgment.

The group shouts at him and the people gather rocks and they throw the rocks at the musician.

SOMEONE
Hey, everybody! There is a struggling writer saying something unique with what appear to be his own original thoughts in just a few blocks away! Let's go!

The group starts to shout and everybody marches away from the musician to the next victim.

HOST
There you have it. Individualistic Facebook post with independent thoughts that no one in the group likes.

A Heavy Metal Band Consisting of Five Talented Babies

VOICE
They are five future women, now in the infancy of their lives.

VOICE
They are a heavy metal band called The Smelly Ones.

VOICE
The group had its first smash hit Writings of the Wall which had one of the greatest lyrics in music history. The first album called Beer Can Motherfucker had five smash hits singles.

The babies play. The fat baby plays guitar with her sausage fingers. The singer sings nonsensical lyrics. The drummer baby hits drums carelessly. The bass player goes away to eat pizza that her mother had brought.

Cellphone Commercial

Here is the cell phone of the future. This cell phone is suited for all people who want communication in the 21st century to be smooth and easy.

This cell phone can also be used to shove it straight into your asshole.

Use the asshole mode and experience the thing that violent American inmates call satisfaction.

Upcoming Books

A stupid, small, comic music plays in the background.

AUTHOR
Thank you and welcome. I am a prolific author you will know for sure. Here is a list of books that I will publish next year.

A thoughtful woman with a quiet, patient voice reveals the names of the books.

The titles are:

Dumb Left-Wing Women – And Other Reasons Why Men Aren't Allowed to Do Anything

I Don't Want a Wise Order, I Want a Pointless Chaos – the History of the Superficial

We Are All Assholes – A Poetic Take on What Humanity Doesn't Talk About

The Metro Suicide of Love – Poems

The Rooms That Lead To Bullshit – A Study on Modern Finnish Youth

It Is Midnight on Facebook and I Can't Get My Dick Out of This Masturbation Machine

Too Drunk to Jerk Off – The History of Eastern Helsinki

The History of Tolerated Evil – What Women Want

Two Men Getting Officially Drunk

Two men are on a cruise in a bar.

MAN 1
Here we are.

Man 2 holds a beer.

MAN 2
An official pleasure – Finnish beer.

MAN 1
Yes indeed.

MAN 2
Soon we will correctly and with great dignity and great behaviour get officially drunk.

MAN 1
Yes, this is an important and official moment.

MAN 2
We are officially having fun and maybe we will use some nice, pure swear words and tell mildly good-natured jokes.

MAN 1
And then we will eat a lot of food like two thoughtful and politically correct nice male humans.

MAN 2
And maybe we will attract two species of the opposite sex and have pre-marital sleeping with them.

MAN 1
And if everything goes alright we will get to touch their private parts. In a polite and gracious, gentlemanly way, of course.

MAN 2
This is a nice and a beautiful, peaceful evening while we will make jokes that are clean and without those horrible masculinity or political incorrectness.

MAN 1
And maybe later we will use our hands to beat men who are violent to us, in a neat and comfortable manner.

MAN 2
Yes, and all our thoughts are filled with cleanliness and sophistication.

MAN 1
Yes, this is clearly a night-out for two single men who have not had the luck to raise the birth rate of our fatherland.

MAN 2
Yes, to do that we must find a clean and nicely behaving young gal who thinks only comfortable thoughts.

MAN 1
And while making love to that woman, the feeling of intercourse feels really nice.

MAN 1
Yes, and we will possibly sing innocent and nice sailor songs in a manner that reminds me of a nice masculine positivity.

MAN 2
Yes. Let's drink. Or consume an alcoholic beverage in a joyous manner.

The men drink.

Wheel of Why Modern Music Sucks

Hello! Welcome to the Wheel of Why Modern Music Sucks! I am your host, Dennis Jordan. Tonight we will have another contest and three guests are quizzed over why modern music indeed sucks. Here our the contestants!

One woman and two men walk by the wheel.

The wheel has these texts on it:

MAX MARTIN
OTHER SWEDISH RECORD PRODUCERS EXCEPT MAX MARTIN
ED SHEERAN'S GENTLE SONGS
ED SHEERAN'S LOUDER SONGS
SOMEONE BEHIND JUSTIN BIEBER
AMERICAN IDOL AND ALL ITS SPIN-OFFS
FEMINISM
MAX MARTIN
SOMEONE BEHIND JUSTIN BIEBER
AMERICAN IDOL AND ALL ITS SPIN-OFFS
AMERICAN IDOL AND ALL ITS SPIN-OFFS
AMERICAN IDOL AND ALL ITS SPIN-OFFS
POLITICAL CORRECTNESS
THE LOSS OF PRINCIPLES AND VALUES

On the wall there are boxes with the unwritten text behind them. The text goes:

- - - -   - - - - -   - - - - - -

THE HOST
Now we'll see on why there is are no true artists in English and American music anymore.

The woman rolls the wheel. It stops at Someone Behind Justin Bieber.

THE HOST
You received 300 bonus points, Susan. Congratulations! What is your guess, Susan?

SUSAN
Fuck Simon Cowell.

THE HOST
Yes, that is correct. You won! This is unprecedented in Wheel of Why Modern Music
Sucks. You must be very excited.

Susan is enjoying her victory and she smiles at the camera.

A Drunken Narcissist to Every Home

THE HOST
Enjoy your own drunken narcissist to your home. He or she will end all your sentences, mock your personality, wound you in many ways possible and ruin your days! Spend only 99,50 euros and you will receive the most irresponsible, bullying asshole to question your every move and ruin your personality.

An aggressive drunken narcissist sits in the living-room with a couple.

THE HOST
The drunken narcissists have three different variations from which you can choose your very special one. There is "The Living Trauma" if you want to be reflected through a woman whose father beat the living fuck out of her. There is "The Irritatingly Evil Lie" for you to never be sane again and to become completely depressed with the help of a menacing and manipulating liar. There is also "The Roaring Meaninglessness" who will hate everything you have ever achieved and bring horror to your soul. Enjoy your very own set of complete and utter evil idiots and you will be unnecessarily traumatized.

A narcissist shouts at everyone in the kitchen.

THE HOST
Please remember: Most of our drunken narcissists are mediocre and untalented musicians who never made it.

Why Do Men Become Hitlers?

Example One

A man is writing his 1000-page novel. He sits by the typewriter and writes manically.

Two months later.

The man is finishing his 1000-page novel. He seems satisfied.

MAN
My 47th book is ready. A thousand pages. I hope I will find more than 20 readers.

The man opens television. He watches a reality show called Temptation Island where the 20 contestants are naked and have a party.

The man growls angrily.

Example Two

A man is a builder. He has built houses and also composed operas and painted great paintings. He watches his paintings in a church.

He reads Shakespeare and Proust and sighs out of amazement. He thinks: "God I love Shakespeare and Proust."

Then he opens television. He watches a reality show called Big Brother where the contestant has pooped himself. The contestant says to everyone: I have pooped myself." The other contestants look at him and say: "Can we see your poop?"

The man sheds his cigar and looks serious. Then he growls angrily.

An Audio Book of James Joyce's Finnegans Wake

THE NARRATOR
Welcome to James Joyce's Finnegans Wake – An Audio Version. I am your narrator,
Glenn Burke.

THE NARRATOR
riverrun, past Eve and Adam's, from swerve of shore to bend of bay, brings us by a
commodius vicus of recirculation back to Howth Castle and Environs.

The narrator is seen reading on a couch.

THE NARRATOR
Sir Tristram, violer d'amores, fr'over the short sea, had passengore rearrived from
North Armorica on this side the scraggy isthmus of Europe Minor to wielderfight his
penisolate war: now had topsawyer's rocks by the stream Oconee exaggerated
themselves to Laurens County's gorgios while they went doublin their mumper all
the….

THE NARRATOR
Time?

The Narrator says: Time?

A man comes by his side and reads the book.

THE MAN
Time. As in a period of passing moments.

THE NARRATOR
Does he really mean time that way? As in a period of passing moments.

THE MAN
I think so.

THE NARRATOR
What? Couldn't he be a bit more accurate?

THE MAN
I don't know. I really don't know.

A Singer of Songs That Are Not Consoling or Comforting

The singer is sitting in a cafeteria with his acoustic guitar.

SINGER
Hi. This is my latest hit called No One Might Listen.

SINGER
You will have a cancer soon…in you smoke too much.
There will be enemies soon…if you live long enough,
Some people will hate you…and pretend to be friendly
I really don't know…if your life will continue gently

You can be a victim of a flood or a terrorist attack
You might wake up in Beijing with a clipped sack
Then the surgeons cannot better your situation
You might get poor and be a street person.

Maybe you will never find love and love will hurt you
By constantly blaming you in a quite a cruel world,
And you might be the victim on a knife attack
Or you may be in a car crash which maims your intestines.

Life can be particularly horrifying to you
And no one might listen
Life can be particularly cruel to you
And no one might listen

A Joke That Only Finnish People Will Initially Understand

THE HOST
Here is a joke that only Finnish people will initially understand.

Two men and one woman, Irmeli, were sitting in a car at night.
Irmeli is a nurse. Irmeli recalled a recent moment from her work
where a fat woman was lying in a jail. The woman had shitted her pants and threw
pieces of her feces at everyone, including Irmeli. Irmeli also said that the woman
had thrown the shit at her from her each individual finger for many times. You know
like from the index finger many times using the thumb to help the throwing of the
shit,
then the middle finger many times, then the ring finger many times…et cetera.

One of the men said: "She goes to work at Trainer's House."

The host laughs and then some unknown men laugh each individually.

Mehmet Uygur – The Empathetic Dictator

THE HOST
Welcome to the country of the world's first empathetic dictator. The president of
Turkistan, Mehmet Uygur. Here we will examine how this dictator uses his gentle
and peace-loving power.

The host walks with the dictator in a concentration camp.

DICTATOR
We always talk to the prisoners. We ask them how much torture they are ready to
experience. And we ask them about their capacity to feel pain.

A woman punches the prisoner's knee softly with a hammer. Then she asks: "Does
this hurt?"

DICTATOR
And then we slightly torture them, some of them. But we always talk to them while
we torture them.

DICTATOR
These are the therapy rooms. They have different functions. The room 1 is for
dissenters and we try to understand why our journalists' want to interfere with the
elections. We discuss current affairs and they talk with us if they want to. We like to
offer a sensitive environment for dissenters and we try to change their way of
thinking into a more healthy and productive manner in which they feel more
comfortable to agree with us.

DICTATOR
The room 2 is for enemies of the state. Many intellectuals and entrepreneurs are here
and we politely argue over which mode of government is better – communism or
capitalism?

INTERVIEWER
I see. Are there any homosexuals here?

DICTATOR
Well, some. We try to massage them and make them watch pictures of naked women,
if they are homosexual men, and pictures of naked men, if they are homosexual
women, or lesbians.

INTERVIEWER
I see. And what do you do with your handicapped and retarded people?

DICTATOR
We usually kill them, fast. I really don't like them that much.

The Rapist Condom

A woman walks down stairs to an underground parking lot where she confronts a big, tall, aggressive rapist.

The rapist attacks her and takes her panties off. The woman yells loudly.

RAPIST
Hey…lady…should I use this one or this one?

WOMAN
What?

The rapist shows a blue condom and a red condom, the condoms aren't yet opened.

RAPIST
These are completely different brands.

Suddenly a commercial is shown.

THE SALESMAN
Yes, if you want to choose fast which condom to use for your particular rape choose Red Lips condom. The rapist condom. They are durable and smooth on the shaft and they extend pleasure to truly criminal and wicked realms. Lots of varieties. Be a good, clean rapist.

The rapist smiles to the camera.

The Guilt-Free Tobacco Commercial

A masculine man with a hat rides a horse.

NARRATOR
If you are a smoker, you are probably dehumanized by your society. Probably your mother wants you to quit. And you want to smoke. And she demonizes you constantly because you smoke. Well, fuck your mother. Also, fuck those warnings which are unnecessary and fascistic. And fuck the neurotic world.

NARRATOR
I hope you smoke a lot. So those fucking health-maniacs will become sensible again.

NARRATOR
Think about the Indians, they invented smoking. And you will become as cool as they.

NARRATOR
Smoking is not nearly as bad as drinking. Have you heard of tobacco drunk drivers or tobacco making someone violent. It never happens.

NARRATOR
Also, many great writers smoke and have smoked. Smoking is great for thinking and writing. Alone, in your comfortable bohemian house where you express yourself in various ways.

NARRATOR
Like Hemingway. He was a cool cat.

NARRATOR
Fuck fascism and smoke.

The masculine man winks at the camera while holding his hat.

Three Characters

Here's the first character. A dangerously obese personal trainer.

A very obese woman tells her client:

"You can eat however much want. I am here for you. Don't listen to those muscular and slim personal trainers. They will only pity you. They only want your money and they make you feel less important. I can smuggle food for you and drinks and candies."

Here's the second character:

A sexually liberated Stephen Hawking

Stephen Hawking goes to a bar and his speech-generating device says to a beautiful woman:

"Do you go here often? I want to strip you and get some of the goodies. I want to play with your tits and get some of that coochie."

Later, six young women are standing in front of Hawking and celebrating.

Here's the third character:

The Mark David Chapman of music

Mark David Chapman stands with his acoustic guitar in front of a microphone.

MARK DAVID CHAPMAN
Hi I'm Mark. I am a lousy and ugly musician. Nowhere near Lennon, qualitatively. I await for some genius musician who talks about peace and is kind to people, to shoot me. It would be nice and it would be good to the world. I also arouse emotions in people who hear my lousy music, they fear that I will kill them like Lennon was killed.

The Events of Which No One Takes a Selfie

1. A woman is having an abortion. Then she asks the abortionist: "I want to take a selfie of this."

The abortionist answers okay.

The woman takes a selfie and her mutilated baby still breathes while she smiles to the camera.

2. A man is kissing his newly wedded wife. Then he watches his wife and thinks: I want to have sex with other women.

The man asks his wife: "Can I take a selfie of this?"

The wife answers yes.

The man takes a selfie and above his head is a thought bubble that says: "I want to have sex with other women."

3. A woman is driving a car and hits a deer.

The woman feels sorry for the dear and takes a selfie of her and the deer. Then she shoots the deer.

The selfie consists of the woman and the deer with the woman saying "I had an accident and I soon had to kill the deer, so sad."

Sane Asylum

THE HOST
There is one aspect of a civilized society, a Western democracy which has been
unknown to the public. Here is a mental health asylum consisting of the sanest people
in that particular society.

Here is Finland's sane asylum. There are many readers here, many unknown authors,
with a lot to say about the modern world.

THE NURSE
We bring the most talented ones of us here to rest. We are very proud of them. There
are intellectuals, artists, renaissance men, spiritual thinkers, poets and autodidacts
here.

THE HOST
How would you describe the patients?

THE NURSE
Lonely people are smart, they find other kindred spirits here. When you think of the
average sane man or woman outside, those who work and form the backbone of our
society, they are really stupid. They have their own Facebook profile and they are
obsessed with sharing every bit of their lives. People tend to be stupid and the
average man is quite dumb. And half of our people are below the average. So the
patients are like a refreshing opposite of them, they don't have to go to work and
work work constantly, they are too clever for it.

THE NURSE
Sometimes we bring the media here, there is so much to discover. Like a fountain of
knowledge and wisdom. Very inspiring.

THE NURSE
We also swap the parts around here. Sometimes a patient asks the nurse about his or
her personal life. There was one moment when the nurse started crying because her
husband beats her. Well, not anymore. We collectively worked on her getting
divorce.

The nurses and the patients yell to the camera:

Bring your talented intellectuals here! Because the public is always behind the age!

Only Sexual Therapists Deserve Sex

SEXUAL THERAPIST
I see. Have you had this sexual dysfunction for how long?

PATIENT
For about five years. My medication does it.

SEXUAL THERAPIST
What do you mean?

PATIENT
I mean that the pills that I take block my sexual potency. I cannot have an orgasm where there is a full ejaculation because my pills stop it. So that is why I don't enjoy masturbation.

SEXUAL THERAPIST
So you have had this problem for five years?

PATIENT
Yes, I tried talking about it to my caretakers, the nurses. But they saw that the pills I take are the last remaining hope that I won't get sick, that I won't be admitted to a mental hospital.

SEXUAL THERAPIST
I see…Well

CUT TO:
A sexual therapist and her husband have passionate, lustful sex on top of a pile of bills.

SEXUAL THERAPIST
Haha, that is how I take money out of my patients. Most of them will remain single. Good for them!

The therapist and her husband laugh together.

Then the therapist swivels in the cash.

They laugh together in a wicked manner.

The Dictator Pizzeria

Two men are awake at night and the other man takes two coffee cups from the
kitchen and they start to drink the coffee.

MAN 1
Have you heard of the Dictator Pizzeria?

MAN 2
What is that?

MAN 1
Well, a pizzeria I went to, had two Turkish men who liked me instantly.
The fat Turkish man was very warm and friendly. He liked me and considered
me a brother, calling me a comrade.

MAN 2
Really?

MAN 1
Yeah, really. And one night, I was with my older brother at the pizzeria and the
fat man heard us talking about the dictators of the world. The pizza men obviously
hated Erdogan, the Turkish dictator. I said something about a Dictator Pizzeria,
that it was my invention. Any how, two months later, as I went to the pizzeria
during night time, there was a film noir playing and the pizza man said to me
bon appétit while he delivered the food for me. I think it was chicken with rice
and with curry sauce.

MAN 2
So? What happened?

MAN 1
Well, I noticed that the pizzeria had names for the pizzas. One name was
Lukashenko. The other was Erdogan and one was Putin.

MAN 2
I see. Interesting. How does this work?

MAN 1
I think each time a pizza is baked, someone in Turkey or in another country will try
to kill the dictator or harm him. It is some kind of a labyrinth, some kind of
psychological warfare. There is a societal freedom that those people yearn. And the

thing is now known in Venezuela and Cuba and this pizza thing, this is the reason why people are now rising up.

MAN 2
So pizza is the key to world peace?

MAN 1
Yes, this is how it seems.

MAN 2
What if you want to buy a drink only? Like a bottle of Pepsi?

MAN 1
Then you will be classed as neutral I guess.

MAN 2
What things did the pizza maker tell you?

MAN 1
He told me: "Welcome to hell." And "I hope you will sleep well."

MAN 2
Charming.

A library on How to Understand Women

THE LIBRARIAN
Welcome to the library on how to understand women. This is a UNESCO'S Heritage
Site.

THE LIBRARIAN
Here we have the sense of humour aisle. There is 26 000 books on how to attract
women with humour. It shows many of the admired techniques and nuanced jokes
that might work on a woman.

THE LIBRARIAN
Here is the aisle concerning masculinity and protection you have to offer a woman.

THE LIBRARIAN
Here is the aisle about women's moods, it consists of 160 000 books. The woman's
body aisle consists of 12 000 books.

THE LIBRARIAN
Here is an aisle on how to attract religious and pious women. And this aisle here is
how to attract scary, powerful women who are exceptionally strong. 160 000 books.

THE LIBRARIAN
Here is one aisle. This is the aisle where we determine how looks affect women. All
the books here show the reader how women don't care for looks and muscular arms
and a six pack. It is called The Liar's Aisle.

THE LIBRARIAN
Here is the Clitoral Aisle. How to satisfy women with your tongue. No books are
needed because it is very easy if you are not a complete idiot.

THE LIBRARIAN
Here we have the final aisle. It is The Jerk Aisle. No books are needed, only one
documentary, on how you only have to be a jerk and prove it.

Grown Man in a Bar with a Baby Girl

A man is sitting opposite a baby girl who looks innocent.

There are about ten other people in a bar where they sit and drink.

MAN
Do you like that juice I bought you?

MAN
Well you don't have to answer that. Cheers!

The man tries to clink his beer glass to the baby girl's juice glass.

MAN
This bar is The Golden Monkey. Do you like that name?

The baby says something unintelligible.

MAN
How old are you?

The baby shows three fingers to him.

MAN
Three? I thought you were two. Well, anyway, my brother, and your father, wanted me to give you a nice time in a bar.

The baby says something unintelligible.

MAN
Yeah, I thinks so too.

Three hours later.

The man is drunk and dances wildly while holding the baby girl in his arms and drinking beer. Dance music plays loudly in the background.

MAN
Are you having a good time, baby?! Are you having a good time?! Wooh!

School Bullies Who Were Killed Later in Life

HOST
This is Marcus. He was a victim of horrifying bullying. Tonight we hear his story as well as the fate of his bullies. Welcome to the show, Marcus.

MARCUS
Thank you.

HOST
What kind of bullying did you experience?

MARCUS
I was beaten and kicked many times. I was also humiliated in front of class many times. The bullies also shared disgusting lies about me which ruined my life for a lot of years.

HOST
What was the worst feeling you had?

MARCUS
The feeling of a live not lived. The feeling that everything goes and nothing happens except pain and sorrow. And the feeling that no one understands you or likes you.

HOST
That's awful, Marcus. Very awful. But now, listen, Marcus, we have a little surprise for you. This was filmed late September. It concerns you bullies.

MARCUS
Really?

HOST
Yes, this video will make you happy again.

The video starts rolling and two men (former bullies) are standing next to an empty car. Suddenly two men arrive from the woods and beat the two bullies to the ground. After that they shoot the bullies many times. They lift the bullies to the trunk.

After this, they drive the car next to the ocean and the bullies are still alive. The men stab the bullies 20 times to assure that they are killed.

After this, the men put the bullies into sacks and throw them into the ocean.

HOST
How do you feel about your life now, Marcus? Didn't we do a great thing for you?

MARCUS
Well, yes. I am grateful.

HOST
Next week we will be talking to another bullied man. His bullies are being tracked and we will find interesting ways to kill them. Good night!

Alcohol Warnings

MAN
I have wondered about the warnings in tobacco products. Did you know they started
to put warnings to alcohol bottles too?

MAN 2
Yes. Finally, something positive. Usually it is smokers who get the blame.

MAN
I happen to have few bottles I purchased a while ago. Let's look at them.

MAN 2
Alright

MAN
This is whiskey, from Scotland. It says: "Warning: a bottle of this stuff is as healthy
to your liver and your throat as someone disembowelling your stomach with a kitchen
knife."

MAN 2
That was a good one.

MAN
Let's see. This is rum from Russia. It says: "If you drink enough of this each day, you
will be able to see your grandchildren ask their parents "Who is that smelly, lonely,
drunken moron?""

MAN 2
I liked that even more.

MAN
And here is the third one. This is English absinthe. It says: "Warning: Drinking this
absinthe will help your heart and your blood vessels become as green as this
absinthe!"

MAN 2
That was okay.

MAN
And finally here is the fourth one. This is vodka from Slovakia. It says: "Drinking
this vodka will create decisions in your brain that will lead you to experience a triple
hangover in the morning."

PART 2

Enjoy Life in a Community

In a community you must think like the others. Like the other young people who hold very fashionable beliefs. Everyone has to agree with everyone.

Opinions you must hold in a community if you want to keep your sanity:

The Greek gods were better than the Christian God (a position held by many young women and needs no facts or explaining to do.)

The breasts of women are neutral, as well as sexuality and passion and other intimate things (which have to be neutralized so that there is no mystique in them.)

Climate change is happening and everyone must believe in it and get anxious over it because the world opinion says so. Also, if you don't believe in it, you will seen as a pariah, an unsocial pariah.

Logic and scepticism are racist. Arguments have to made emotionally and forcefully so that no one suspects their basis or their critical thinking.

Every girl and every woman are completely wise and perfect from the beginning (a position that needs no explanation even though at least 50 percent of girls and women make serious moral mistakes, and tend not to regret them.)

Seriousness and sophistication are scary things. There is something suspicious about young men and women who won't get drunk and who believe in good behaviour and good morality.

You must not have a sexual morality. You only must feel bitterness and guilt over not jumping to the sexual game where everyone has to have 12-50 partners before they reach 30.

Opinions That No One Holds These Days

"I have to admit. I really like consumerism and materialism. They make me happy!"

"I think the constant talk about the need to lose one's ego is such nonsense. Why is ego so bad?"

"I really don't like modern entertainment and I don't want to be a part of it in any way."

"I really do feel that one is better with staying home than going to work."

"I like to read and analyze classic poems that are over 50 pages long."

"I think there is not enough people in the world. I hope every nation has a lot of new-born babies."

"I really hate people who haven't suffered much and are therefore very shallow human beings."

Hockey Audience Member

Two teams are playing an aggressive and rough hockey game.

A thin and long male is watching the game. He has glasses.

Next to him is a masculine and rough man yelling and shouting.

The thin and long male starts to ask questions from the hockey players by shouting to them.

THE MALE
Hey, I really enjoy how you play hockey! It makes me feel good! Remember how well Dostoevsky wrote The Karamazov Brothers! He had a flow and he wrote beautifully a novel which is almost a thousand pages long! I would like you to play your sport like the famous Russian writer wrote his novels! He was really good at writing novels!

The masculine man looks at the thin and long man and finds him weird.

THE MALE
Yeah, keep playing as well as Dostoevsky! And remember Tchaikovsky's great ballet, Swan Lake! He was very cunning and ingenious at composing! Not to mention that he wrote The Waltz of Flowers! I think it's about women! Because I saw a YouTube video where there was flowers and it reminded me of vaginas! Like every woman's vagina is like a flowers blooming!

One hockey player tackles the other hockey player brutally.

THE MALE
Oh, no! Please don't indulge in that kind of behaviour! I like hockey when it is less violent! The defence player of that team which has yellow and blue team jackets skates like a figure skater! It is very beautiful and elegant, like Proust's Remembrance of Things Past! I really like his skating! I think he is going to be a great player! I also liked his goal which he scored twenty minutes ago! It was a very beautiful goal!

The Hockey Scientist and The Music Professor

NEWS ANCHOR
The Finnish national hockey league has hired a prestigious hockey scientist to their organization.

The hockey scientist knows everything about hockey even though he has never played the sport.

The hockey scientist knows all the strategies, the offences, the power play patterns and all the schemes that the players make in modern hockey.

He has also examined the velocity of the puck and the surface of the ice so that he knows all the ways the puck will move in a given situation.

The Finnish national hockey league is grateful for its new member.

NEWS ANCHOR
It was The Grammy's again. The biggest music awards show in the world was held yesterday night. The most central awards went to The Music Professor. He is a 55-year old man who has been called a musical elitist. The Music Professor creates music with his brain and composed three thousand smash hits in last year alone. He is considered the brains of music and has been called The Garri Kasparov of melodies.

The Music Professor goes to the stage to receive his award. He moves to the microphone in a wagon while giving the middle finger to the audience. After receiving his award, he moves to backstage in a wagon while giving the middle finger to the audience.

Is School Necessary?

A man is seduced by a very beautiful woman.

The man has sex with her.

The woman says to him he is the most physically exceptional lover she has ever had.

They get married and celebrate their marriage on Instagram.

They get 1,100 likes on that particular post.

Then the man goes with a jet plane to Vienna to a mansion to have a party with his friends.

They are all happy and play music from YouTube.

They walk on the mansion and drink alcohol and they are ecstatic.

The man has sex with five beautiful women on the jet plane when he returns to Finland.

The man is re-united with his wife. The wife has written on Instagram how much she misses him and how special he is.

The man finds a thousand dollar bill in a bush and takes it.

Then the man and his wife have pleasurable sex.

Next week, the wife says to him: "I'm pregnant."

They celebrate the pregnancy and the man hugs the wife and the wife kisses him.

Then the dream is over.

A 13-year old, bullied, fat boy wakes up sleepy.

His mother yells at him: "Come on, go to school!"

The boy answers: "I don't want to. I am bullied there. I hate school!"

The mother drags the boy aggressively and the boy cries.

At the school, five bullies throw pieces of snus to the boy.

The boy thinks: "Fuck."

Finland – The Happiest Country on Earth

NEWS ANCHOR
Finland is generally considered the happiest country on planet Earth. We thought of making an investigative documentary on this issue. We sent our best documentarian to see how happy are Finland as a people. Here's how it went:

The documentarian sits with two aggressive young women and one man on the grass.

The young, apathetic man throws up on the grass. He holds a beer.

The women look nihilistic and cold.

Then the documentarian is visiting a bar in Pispala.

He politely talks to people there. Everyone else is unfortunately aggressive and dumb-sounding.

He talks with a young woman. Then he politely asks the young woman outside.

Outside, an old, ugly and scary woman says unintelligible nonsense in a very obnoxious way. The woman laughs at the man and is frighteningly abrasive.

Then the documentarian goes to walk on the street. He asks a slovenly and poor-looking man who drinks beer while sitting on the street: "Can I help you?"

The man answers: "No, fuck you and go fucking die, you fuck!"

Then the documentarian is in a public swimming pool and he finds a man shitting in the water. The documentarian is appalled and leaves the swimming pool.

Then the documentarian is enjoying the night life in Hervanta smoking a cigarette outside but then the police and the ambulance arrive. The police arrest a man who says he jumped from the balcony but survived and a woman who says she got stabbed by the man.

They shout a lot of unintelligible things because they are afraid of going to jail. Then they are forced into an ambulance and a police car.

Celebrity Survey

Here is a piece called Celebrity Survey. We asked some celebrities bunch of stuff and we got the answers. Here are the questions:

The moment I realized I was a jerk.

Madonna wrote:

When I had said bad things about my friend.

Kim Kardashian wrote:

When I, as a rich woman, forgot the plight of the poor and the needy.

Donald Trump wrote:

When I was a sperm in my father's testicles.

Here's a new one.

The greatest achievement of my career was:

Richard Dawkins wrote:

When I wrote my books about the wonders of the natural world.

Elon Musk wrote:

When I became the Product Architect of Tesla, Inc.

Vanilla Ice wrote:

Last year, when I became a dishwasher.

Here's another one.

The trait that makes me such a great actor is:

Tom Hanks wrote:

My sensible, masculine presence.

Leonardo DiCaprio wrote:

My talent for playing different kinds of characters.

Charlie Sheen wrote:

Not being Charlie Sheen.

What do I like to do in my spare time?

Angela Merkel wrote:

Watch television and enjoy different kinds of nice programs.

Boris Johnson wrote:

Drink beer with my friends.

Vladimir Putin wrote:

Strangling a close friend by staring at him.

Actual Items

We found some commercials. And we thought they were innocent. But there was weird texts under them which we found weird and want to show.

Here is a peanut commercial. A nice commercial.

But look what it says under it:

"Nice food to die of boredom while you watch nine hours of political debate."

Here is an orange commercial. It seems innocent.

But look what is under it:

"These fruits are juicier than transsexual mother's milk ducts."

Here is a commercial selling fans. Fans are nice, they freshen up the air.

But look what it says under it:

"Helps to clean the air after a nine-hour insomniac night of tending your baby."

Here is a toilet seat commercial. It seems nice.

But look what it says under it:

"Elvis died on one of these."

Here is a bicycle commercial. Again, it seems so nice.

But look what is said under it:

"Ride a bicycle downhill and crash into a pedestrian. I assure you, the pedestrian will not like it."

Here is nice commercial of a jigsaw puzzle.

Look what it says under it:

"Build a jigsaw puzzle for five hours and you will lose five hours of hot, steamy sex with a fashion model."

Here is a commercial of marinated chicken. It seems nice.

But look what it says under it:

"These chickens died in vain."

Here is a commercial for an electric scooter.

Look what it says underneath:

"Makes old people with walkers look like idiots."

Here is an apple commercial.

Look what it says under it:

"The least likable of all fruits."

Christian Pornography

We are here to interview two Christian porn stars and we will study
the whole new phenomenon called Christian pornography. These porn stars
are married to one another and love each other. They are both Roman Catholics.
I think we will all be surprised by this phenomenon and this will be an interesting
interview.

The man is in a room with two Christian porn stars, a man and a woman.

What kind of pornography is your Christian pornography?

Well, there is a lot of cuddling. And a lot of hugging. And kissing. Between two
adults who are already married. And kissing happens only when the clothes are on.
There is no nudity. These videos last ten to twenty minutes and there is a lot of
nuance in these. The viewer will love the sensuality of these human relationships
under Christ. Of course we hope that the viewers are Christian and won't masturbate
while watching our videos. We only hope they will be aroused in positive and healthy
ways.

What do you want to achieve with this pornography?
We want to spread the message of faith-based love and Christian sensuality.

Are there also fetishes?

There are fetishes, but not in our videos. Other videos have fetishes like "A Christian
woman converts me to Christianity and then has sex with me."

And "A Christian woman says Jesus loves me but also wants to have sex with me."

Are there rougher versions of Christian porn?

Yes there are. Like a Baptist blow job and Episcopalian 69. And of course the
Missionary Position.

There is also gay porn for Christians. That is quite popular with the men who want to
cure their gay clients.

There is also retard porn. That is reserved for people who believe in Creationism.

Lying Scum Shit Bag Asshole Gross Disgusting Jackass

This man is a famous businessman who inherited his fortune from his father.

He shoots squirrels just for the fun of it. He also tortures hedgehogs and little birds.

He has even lied about his son being a retard just to get women's sympathy for him.

He eats five hamburgers a day and enjoys thinking about cattle that suffered because of it.

When his mother was on her deathbed, he said to the mother that he hopes that she will die soon and said: "Eat more butter."

He also made jokes and laughed at Dachau Concentration Camps and never regretted it. He even bought a shirt where it says I love Dachau and smiled and gave a thumb in a photograph with it.

He has offended women, the disabled, all ethnic minorities, transgendered, gays and just people who seem weak.

He often goes to someone's front yard and offending the guy for no reason.

He has beat his ex-wife and blamed her for leaving him.

He always enjoys being arrogant and bad just for the fun of it. He never cares about how much his words and actions hurt others.

When he was part of a group visiting a young man's deceased sister, the young man cried a lot on the grave, but this jackass smiled and laughed at the young man who missed his sister.

He lies approximately ten times per hour, sometimes even more. He likes to lie.

And he has everything.

Think about that.

Things That Never Happened in History

1962, Robert F. Kennedy phones John F. Kennedy who is staying in a hotel.

ROBERT F. KENNEDY
Hi, Jack!

JOHN F. KENNEDY
Hi, Bobby! What's going on?

ROBERT F. KENNEDY
Things are going great.

JOHN F. KENNEDY
Great. I was with Marilyn two days ago.

ROBERT F. KENNEDY
Yes, I heard about it.

JOHN F. KENNEDY
Yeah.

ROBERT F. KENNEDY
So how was Marilyn?

JOHN F. KENNEDY
She was great. Her ass was nice and big and it gave my penis a great immovable object to rub my foreskin and jerk my penis until I came.

ROBERT F. KENNEDY
Yeah, I know that feeling. I had sex with her just like that but she also rode me and her thighs moved so fast left and right that I came almost instantly. I also banged her the second time and didn't let her out of the house because I played for two hours with her tits and ass.

JOHN F. KENNEDY
Great, we have both enjoyed her now. Now I have to go and write a speech. See you later, bro!

The Three Things I'm Tired Of – An Audio Sketch

1

I'm tired of these pointless idiots who think their shallow, insignificant thoughts are poetry.

They are writing some kind of boring thought flow without words that have either meaning or aesthetic significance. They just write whatever comes to their minds and publish one poem a day while me, a genuine, significant and great poet, write only two or three poems a month, at least.

Poets, you need to have something original, beautiful and unique to write about.

Then you encrust your poem with interesting words and exciting sentences.

Also the subject should be clear and the emotion should be significant.

There is no time for shitty poets.

2

I'm also tired of this fucking ultra-egalitarian leftist bullshit notion that everybody is multi-talented and special and that everybody has an important voice in the artistic field.

Bullshit!

There are clear distinctions in art. There are, in music, movies and books. Greatness is greatness, fuck you. Usually individualistic and independent from what the public thinks. The rest is usually mediocre or shit.

Nowadays the mediocre are called the genius and the genius are called the mediocre.

These ultra-egalitarian fuck heads, usually women, see music, movies and books, without any kind of common sense or philosophy of life or a thinking mind. They are not thinkers. They salivate and hype over everybody's shitty new song or mediocre poem just because they are women and friends with them.

It hurts true artists.

3

I am getting really tired of love being used as a force, in an argument.

These debaters are always the most controlling and cold-hearted people. They don't even debate. They use love as a weapon, as a verb and as the greatest of all virtues.

Love is not the greatest of all virtues. It is an emotion and a collective or individual power. But it certainly doesn't ensure goodness.

People think love for everyone is some kind of a duty. One should love everyone, at least try to.

I don't love everyone. I hate many aspects of the human condition because the human condition is generally immoral. People usually make everything as hard and as difficult and cruel as it can be. Humanity is more like a jungle and I generally hope it is a church.

But it is not. Pretending that everyone loves everyone, is a moral fallacy, which doesn't admit the cruelties and horrifying mistakes that people commit on a daily basis.

I also don't think everyone wants to be with everyone for a particularly long time. These people think so, or at least pretend so.

The Mind-Blowing Things About Life

When you are sitting on a couch, hundreds of millions of people are driving a car and experience an active, action-filled succession of moments, i.e. the present or the day in different places at the same time.

While you were five years old you went to a day-care centre. When you are 32 years old, you watch the photograph of all the kids together. And you don't know what you thought during the photograph.

Have you ever found out that someone you knew in adulthood, was actually in the same school that you went as a 7-11-year old, 20 years ago?

Have you ever found out that your best friend in adulthood, was actually in high school, 20 years ago, while you went the junior high school next to it?

Have you ever watched 3000 photographs from the 1990s when you were a child, and the photographs have a total life of their own, so much life. Then you see your present day, as 32 years old, and you are alone and nothing is usually happening anymore. It is like a land that exists no more.

When Clint Eastwood was 14 years old, in 1944, Adolf Hitler hadn't shot himself yet.

In 1990 there was no Facebook, Twitter, YouTube and Instagram. Nowadays most of the humanity uses them to express themselves.

What did John F. Kennedy dream the night before his death in Dallas, Texas?